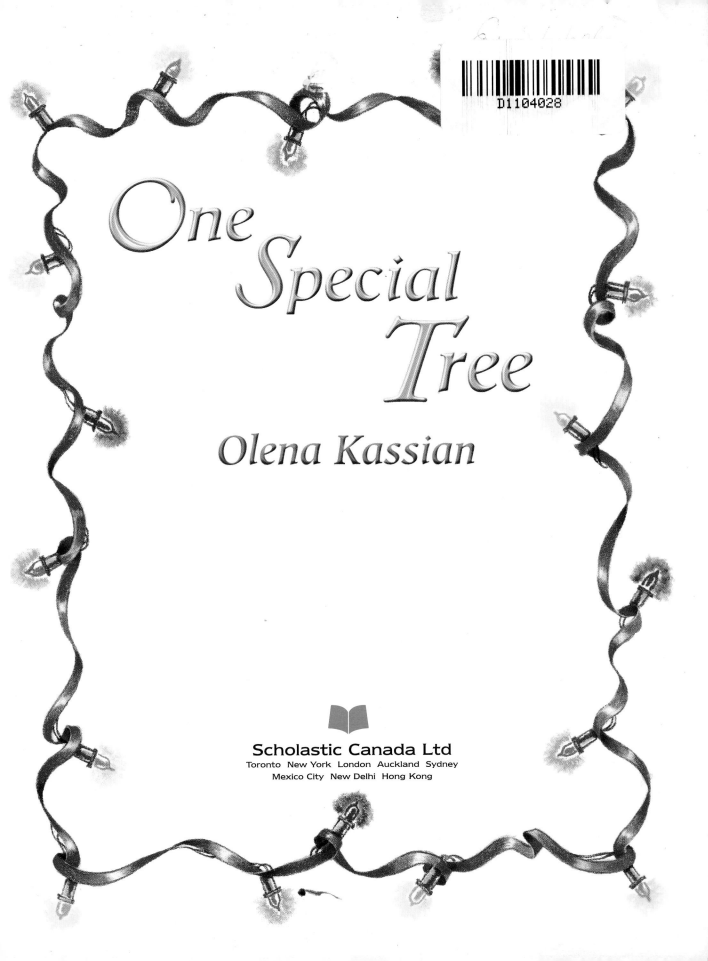

One Special Tree

Olena Kassian

Scholastic Canada Ltd
Toronto New York London Auckland Sydney
Mexico City New Delhi Hong Kong

Dedicated to my parents, Roman and Marika Kassian,
who provided the models for the thoughtful mother and father in this book.

The artwork for each picture is prepared using hard and soft pastels on Wallis Sanded Pastel Paper.

This book was designed in QuarkXPress, with type set in 15 point ITC Tiffany.

Scholastic Canada Ltd.
175 Hillmount Road., Markham, Ontario L6C 1Z7 Canada

Scholastic Inc.
555 Broadway, New York, NY 10012, USA

Scholastic Australia Pty Limited
PO Box 579, Gosford, NSW 2250, Australia

Scholastic New Zealand Limited
Private Bag 94407, Greenmount, Auckland, New Zealand

Scholastic Ltd.
Villiers House, Clarendon Avenue, Leamington Spa,
Warwickshire CV32 5PR, UK

Canadian Cataloguing in Publication Data

Kassian, Olena
One special tree

Trade edition ISBN 0-439-98767-9
School edition ISBN 0-439-98747-4
I. Title.

PS8571.A866O53 2000   jC813'.54   C00-931229-3
PZ7.K37Pe 2000

5 4 3 2 1   Printed and bound in Canada   0 1 2 3 4 /0

I'll never forget the Christmas of The Tree.

It started out like any other Christmas. Outside, a deep quilting of snow made the world seem quiet and peaceful. Inside, our excitement was growing. There was so much to do, and so much to look forward to! Like buying our tree.

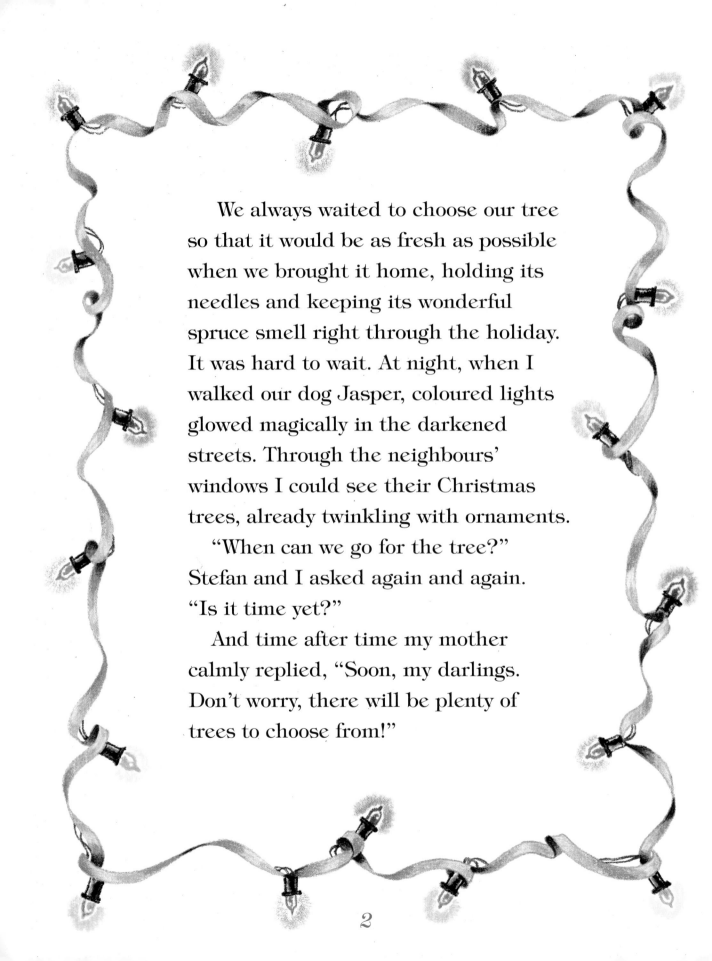

We always waited to choose our tree
so that it would be as fresh as possible
when we brought it home, holding its
needles and keeping its wonderful
spruce smell right through the holiday.
It was hard to wait. At night, when I
walked our dog Jasper, coloured lights
glowed magically in the darkened
streets. Through the neighbours'
windows I could see their Christmas
trees, already twinkling with ornaments.

"When can we go for the tree?"
Stefan and I asked again and again.
"Is it time yet?"

And time after time my mother
calmly replied, "Soon, my darlings.
Don't worry, there will be plenty of
trees to choose from!"

I passed the corner lot every day on my way home from school, and peered through the fence at the trees for sale there. Some were so big they would have filled our small living room, others so tall they could have pierced the ceiling. But I knew there was one among them that would be just right for us. There always was.

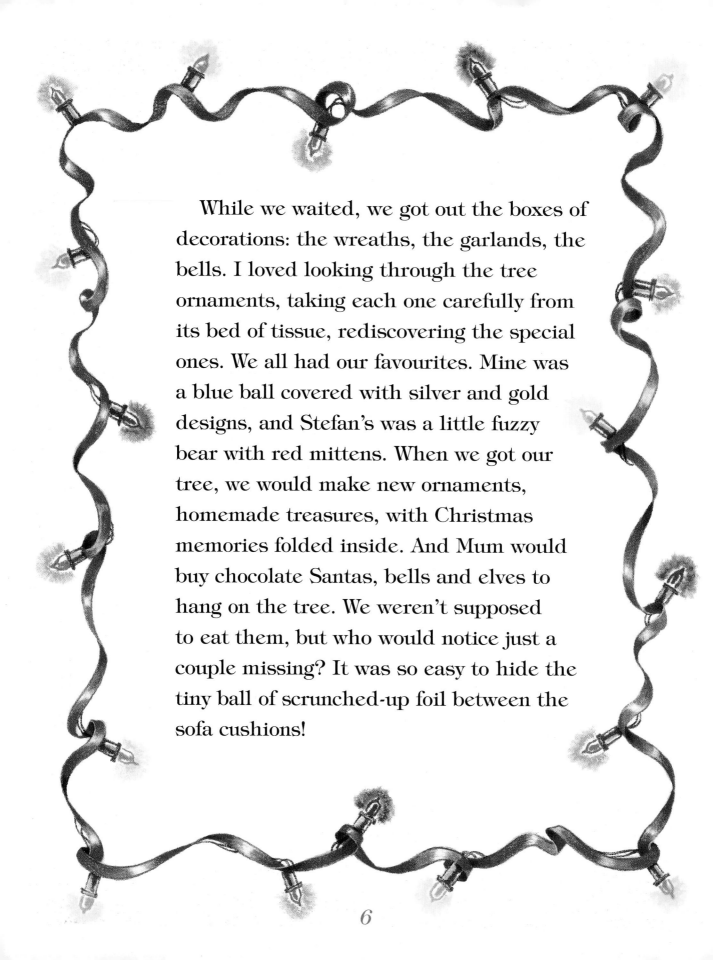

While we waited, we got out the boxes of decorations: the wreaths, the garlands, the bells. I loved looking through the tree ornaments, taking each one carefully from its bed of tissue, rediscovering the special ones. We all had our favourites. Mine was a blue ball covered with silver and gold designs, and Stefan's was a little fuzzy bear with red mittens. When we got our tree, we would make new ornaments, homemade treasures, with Christmas memories folded inside. And Mum would buy chocolate Santas, bells and elves to hang on the tree. We weren't supposed to eat them, but who would notice just a couple missing? It was so easy to hide the tiny ball of scrunched-up foil between the sofa cushions!

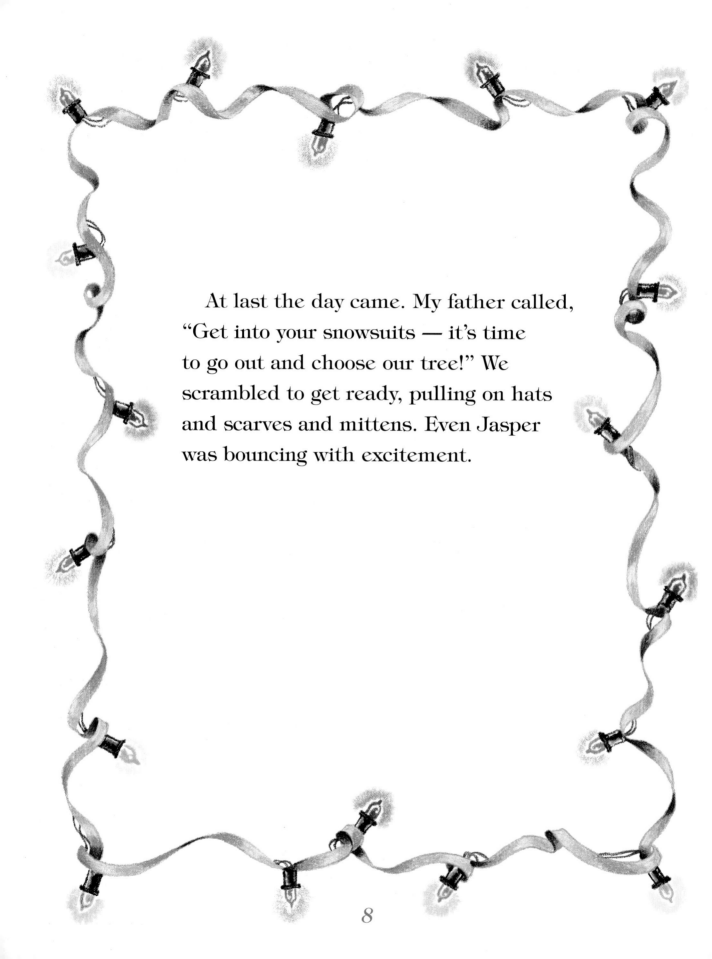

At last the day came. My father called,
"Get into your snowsuits — it's time
to go out and choose our tree!" We
scrambled to get ready, pulling on hats
and scarves and mittens. Even Jasper
was bouncing with excitement.

When we arrived at the lot, Stefan and Jasper and I ran through the trees, looking for the perfect spruce — full, but not too full, just tall enough, and nicely branched so that the ornaments would show well.

Mum and Dad pulled trees out one by one, turning them carefully, comparing, judging. Stefan got tired of looking at trees and started playing hide and seek with Jasper. I wandered off toward the back of the lot. Was that where they kept the best trees, the ones for special customers like us?

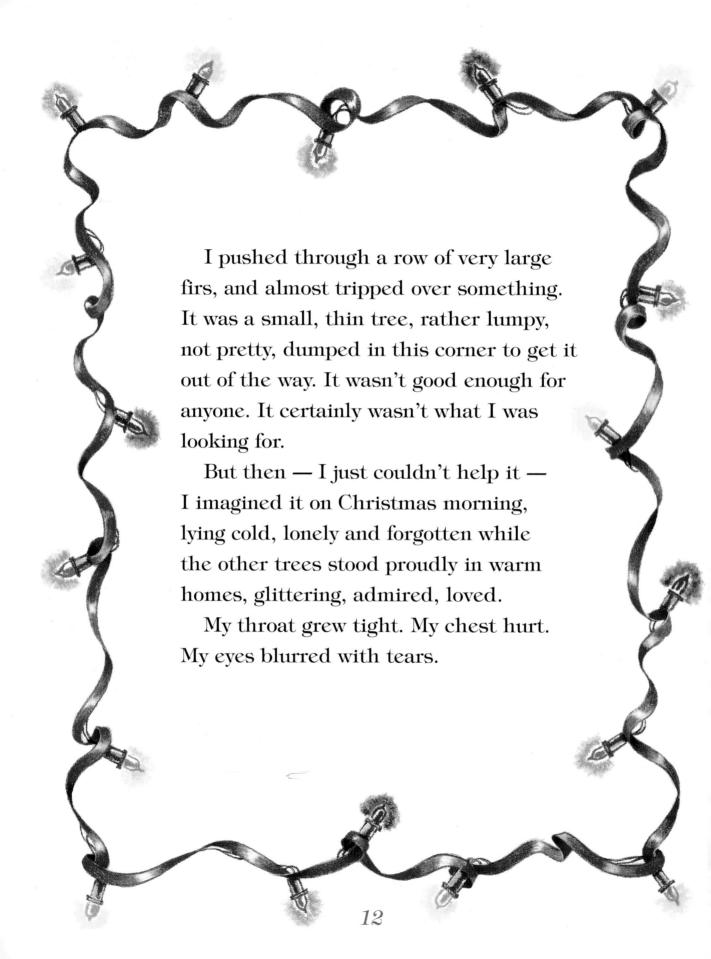

I pushed through a row of very large
firs, and almost tripped over something.
It was a small, thin tree, rather lumpy,
not pretty, dumped in this corner to get it
out of the way. It wasn't good enough for
anyone. It certainly wasn't what I was
looking for.

But then — I just couldn't help it —
I imagined it on Christmas morning,
lying cold, lonely and forgotten while
the other trees stood proudly in warm
homes, glittering, admired, loved.

My throat grew tight. My chest hurt.
My eyes blurred with tears.

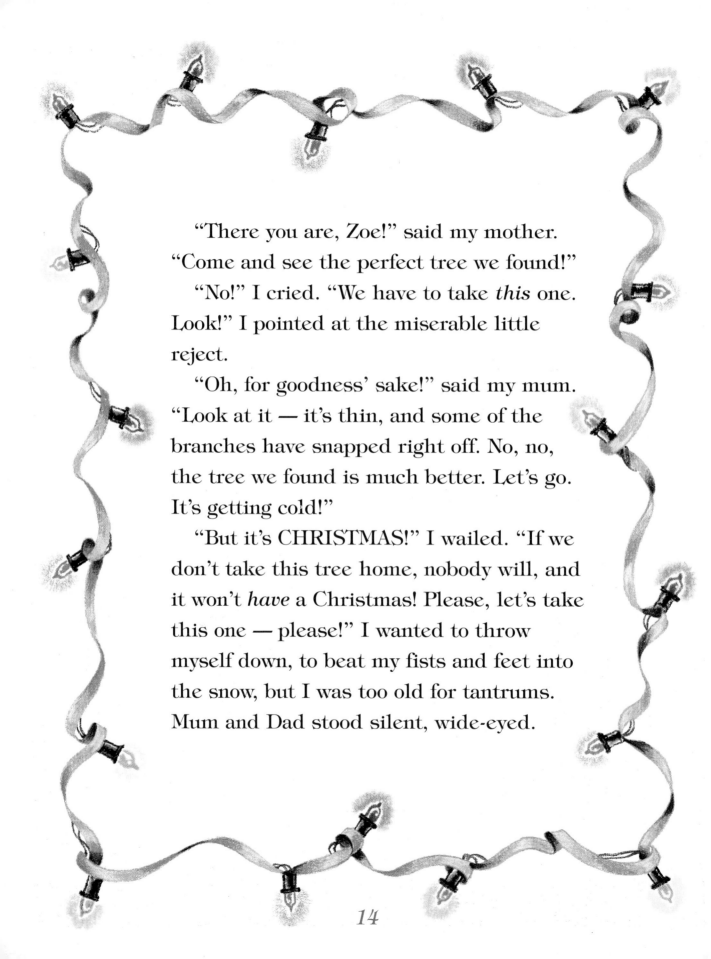

"There you are, Zoe!" said my mother. "Come and see the perfect tree we found!"

"No!" I cried. "We have to take *this* one. Look!" I pointed at the miserable little reject.

"Oh, for goodness' sake!" said my mum. "Look at it — it's thin, and some of the branches have snapped right off. No, no, the tree we found is much better. Let's go. It's getting cold!"

"But it's CHRISTMAS!" I wailed. "If we don't take this tree home, nobody will, and it won't *have* a Christmas! Please, let's take this one — please!" I wanted to throw myself down, to beat my fists and feet into the snow, but I was too old for tantrums. Mum and Dad stood silent, wide-eyed.

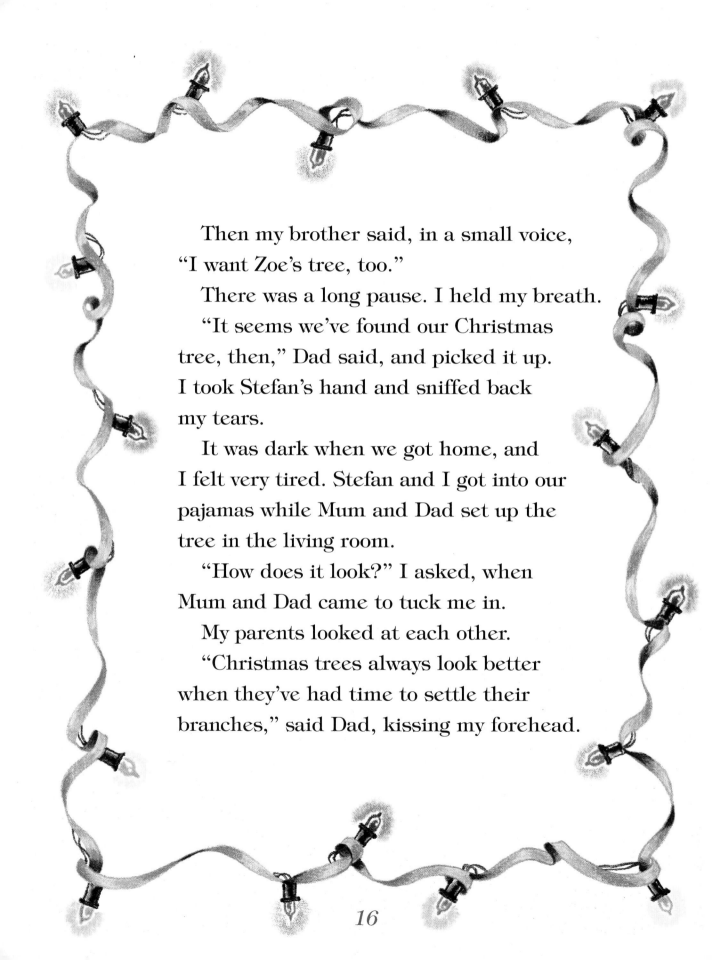

Then my brother said, in a small voice, "I want Zoe's tree, too."

There was a long pause. I held my breath.

"It seems we've found our Christmas tree, then," Dad said, and picked it up. I took Stefan's hand and sniffed back my tears.

It was dark when we got home, and I felt very tired. Stefan and I got into our pajamas while Mum and Dad set up the tree in the living room.

"How does it look?" I asked, when Mum and Dad came to tuck me in.

My parents looked at each other.

"Christmas trees always look better when they've had time to settle their branches," said Dad, kissing my forehead.

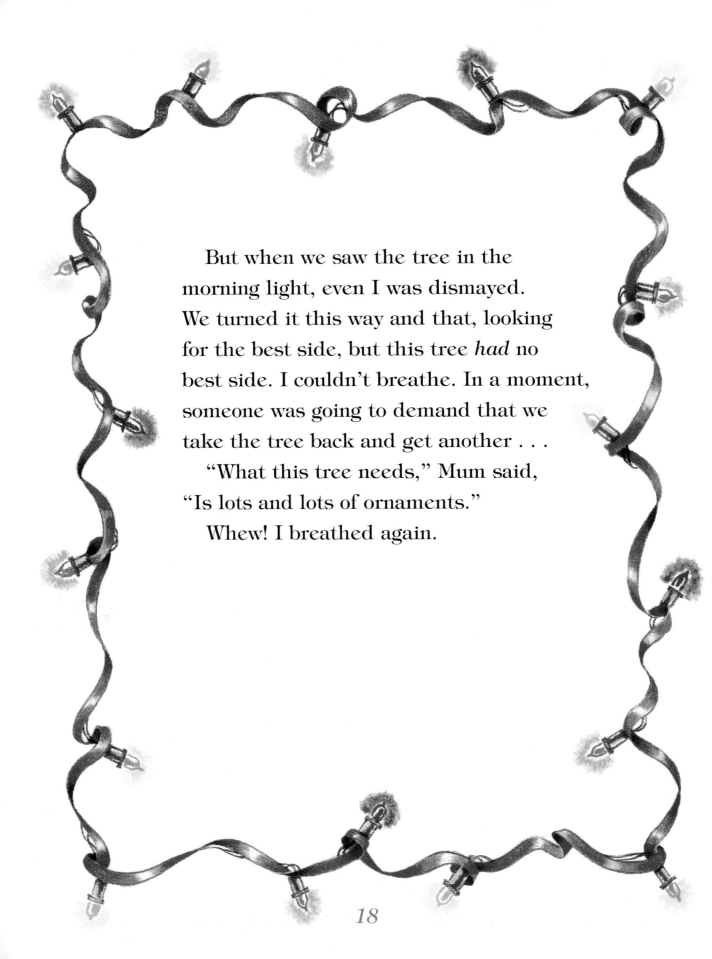

But when we saw the tree in the
morning light, even I was dismayed.
We turned it this way and that, looking
for the best side, but this tree *had* no
best side. I couldn't breathe. In a moment,
someone was going to demand that we
take the tree back and get another . . .

"What this tree needs," Mum said,
"Is lots and lots of ornaments."

Whew! I breathed again.

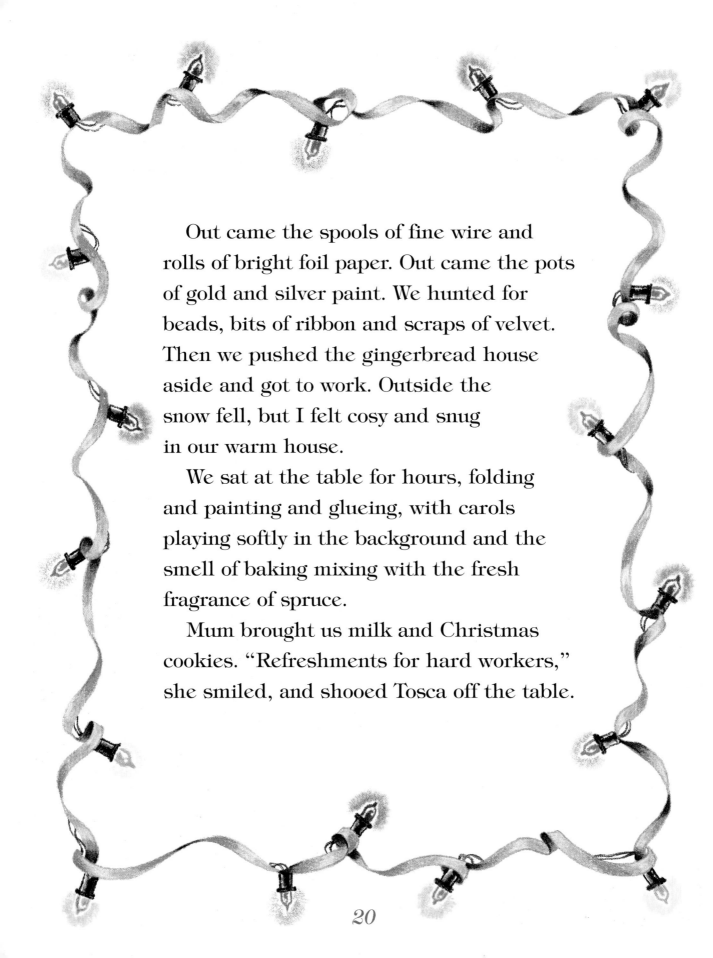

Out came the spools of fine wire and rolls of bright foil paper. Out came the pots of gold and silver paint. We hunted for beads, bits of ribbon and scraps of velvet. Then we pushed the gingerbread house aside and got to work. Outside the snow fell, but I felt cosy and snug in our warm house.

We sat at the table for hours, folding and painting and glueing, with carols playing softly in the background and the smell of baking mixing with the fresh fragrance of spruce.

Mum brought us milk and Christmas cookies. "Refreshments for hard workers," she smiled, and shooed Tosca off the table.

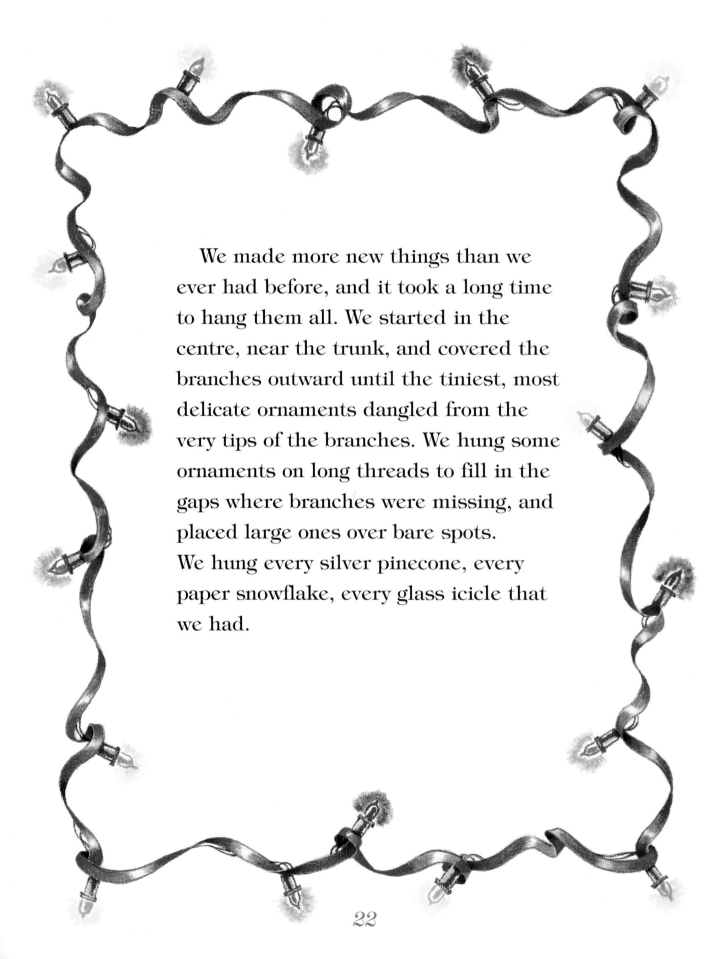

We made more new things than we ever had before, and it took a long time to hang them all. We started in the centre, near the trunk, and covered the branches outward until the tiniest, most delicate ornaments dangled from the very tips of the branches. We hung some ornaments on long threads to fill in the gaps where branches were missing, and placed large ones over bare spots. We hung every silver pinecone, every paper snowflake, every glass icicle that we had.

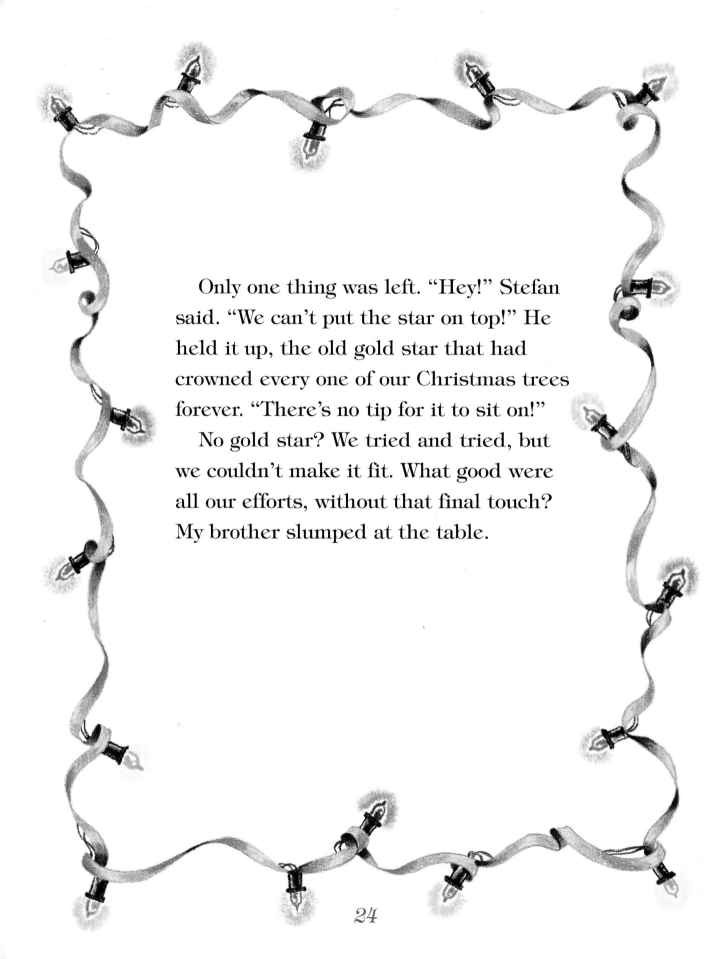

Only one thing was left. "Hey!" Stefan said. "We can't put the star on top!" He held it up, the old gold star that had crowned every one of our Christmas trees forever. "There's no tip for it to sit on!"

No gold star? We tried and tried, but we couldn't make it fit. What good were all our efforts, without that final touch? My brother slumped at the table.

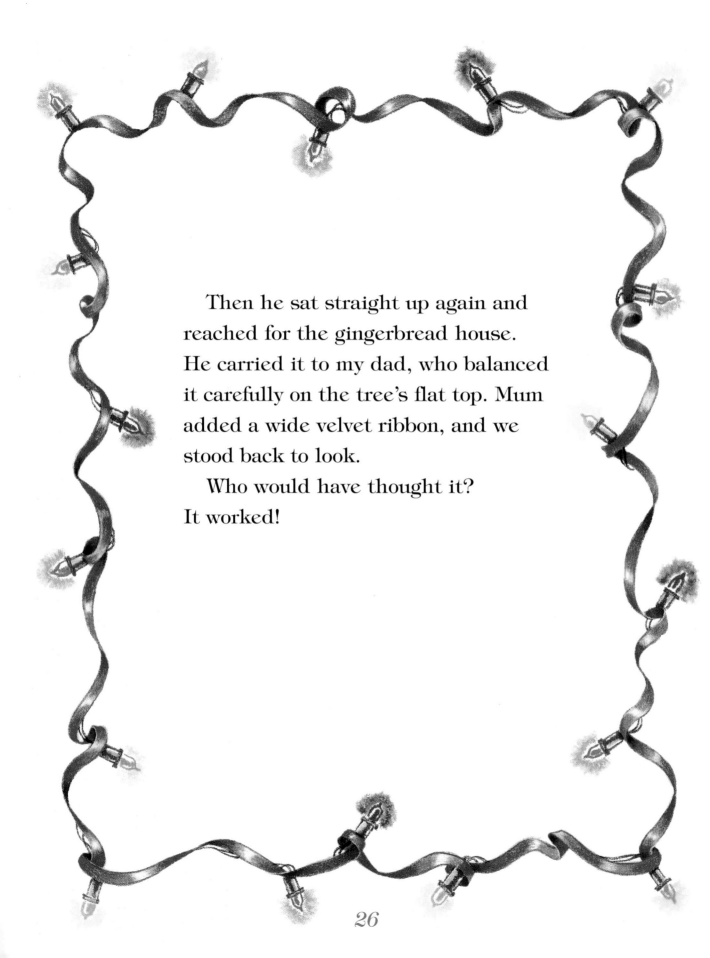

Then he sat straight up again and reached for the gingerbread house. He carried it to my dad, who balanced it carefully on the tree's flat top. Mum added a wide velvet ribbon, and we stood back to look.

Who would have thought it?
It worked!

Our special tree was finished.
It wasn't perfect, but oh, it was BEAUTIFUL!

How to make Zoe and Stefan's Snowflake Ornament

Materials:

Wrapping or craft paper

Ruler

Scissors

Stapler

Tape

- Cut a piece of paper about 18 x 30 cm (heavy foil wrapping paper works well).

- On the short side, make a fold about 2 cm deep. Continue to fold, accordion-style, until the whole paper is folded. If you're using wrapping paper, the coloured side should show on both sides — if you have extra paper, trim it off.

- Fold the accordion in half, to make a crease.

- Put a staple along the crease.

- Now cut 2 or 3 small triangles into each folded side of the accordion, on both sides of the staple, to make your snowflake. Don't cut too much away, or your snowflake will fall apart.

- Trim the ends at an angle.

- Gently open the snowflake into a circle and tape the open edges together on the back of the snowflake.

- Thread a ribbon or string through one of the holes, and your snowflake is ready to hang on the tree!

Tip:
If you make the same pattern of cuts on both sides of the staple, your snowflake will be symmetrical like a real snowflake.